And a
NOOK GASE
in my
BOOK CASE

BOOK CLUB EDITION

There's a WOCKET in my POCKET !

There's a WOCKET in my POCKET!

By Dr. Seuss

A Bright & Early Book
From BEGINNER BOOKS
A Division of Random House, Inc., New York

Copyright © 1974 by Dr. Seuss and A.S. Geisel. All rights reserved under International and Pan-American Copyright Conventions. Published in the United States by Random House, Inc., New York, and simultaneously in Canada by Random House of Canada Limited, Toronto. Library of Congress Cataloging in Publication Data: Seuss, Dr. There's a wocket in my pocket! (A Bright & early book, 18) SUMMARY: A household of unusual creatures help beginning readers recognize common "household" words. [1. Stories in rhyme] I. Title. PZ8.3.G276Tg [E] 74-5516 ISBN 0-394-82920-4 ISBN 0-394-92920-9. (lib. bdg.). Manufactured in the United States of America.

Did you
ever have the feeling
there's a
WASKET
in your
BASKET?

...Or a NUREAU
in your BUREAU?

. . . Or a WOSET in your CLOSET?

Sometimes
I feel quite CERTAIN
there's a JERTAIN
in the CURTAIN.

Sometimes
I have the feeling
there's a ZLOCK
behind the CLOCK.

And that ZELF
up on that SHELF!

I have
talked to him
myself.

That's the
kind of house
I live in.

There's a NINK
in the SINK.

And a
ZAMP
in the
LAMP.

And they're
rather nice
. . . I think.

Some of them
are very friendly.

Like the
YOT
in the
POT.

But
that
YOTTLE
in
the
BOTTLE!

Some are friendly.
Some are NOT.

I like the
ZABLE
on the
TABLE.

And the
GHAIR under the CHAIR.

But that BOFA
    on the SOFA . . .

Well,
I wish
he wasn't there.

All those NUPBOARDS
in the CUPBOARDS.

They're good fun
to have about.

But that
NOOTH GRUSH
on my
TOOTH BRUSH...

Him
I could
do without!

The only one
I'm really scared of
is   that   VUG
under the RUG.

And that QUIMNEY
up the CHIMNEY . . .

I don't like him.
Not at all.

And it makes me sort of nervous
when the ZALL scoots down the HALL.

But the YEPS
on the STEPS—

They're great fun
to have around.

And so are
many, many
other friends
that I have found. . . .

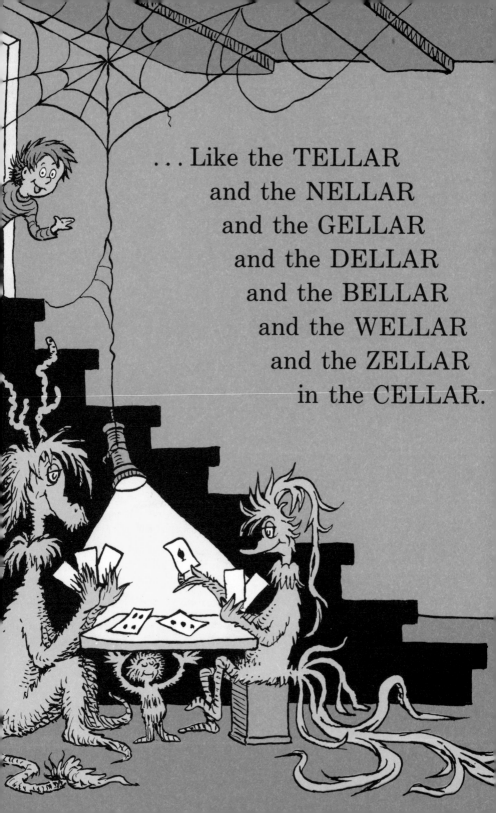

. . . Like the TELLAR
and the NELLAR
and the GELLAR
and the DELLAR
and the BELLAR
and the WELLAR
and the ZELLAR
in the CELLAR.

...And the GEELING
on the CEILING...

.. and
the
ZOWER
in
my
SHOWER ...

. . . and the ZILLOW
    on my PILLOW.

    I don't care
    if you believe it.
    That's the kind of house
    I live in.
    And I hope
    we never leave it.

A FINDOW
in my
WINDOW